To Mum and Dad - for your constant
enthusiasm and unwavering belief — C.B.

Merry Christmas, Rosie — K.H.

First published 2019 by Macmillan Children's Books
an imprint of Pan Macmillan,
The Smithson, 6 Briset Street, London, EC1M 5NR
Associated companies throughout the world
www.panmacmillan.com

ISBN: 978-1-5098-7988-5

Text copyright © Carys Bexington 2019
Illustrations copyright © Kate Hindley 2019

1 2 3 4 5 6 7 8 9

A CIP catalogue record for this book is available
from the British Library.

Printed in China.

Written by
CARYS BEXINGTON

Illustrated by
KATE HINDLEY

THE
NIGHT BEFORE
CHRISTMAS
IN
WONDERLAND

MACMILLAN CHILDREN'S BOOKS

'Twas the night before Christmas, a dark snowy night
When St Nick and his reindeer were just taking flight.
His sleigh was jam-packed, brimming over with toys
To deliver that eve to the good girls and boys.

He took up his reins, breathed in gulps of good cheer
And called to his team, as he did every year,
"Go Dasher! Go Dancer! On Prancer and Vixen!
Leap Cupid! Soar Donner! Fly Comet and Blitzen!"

But suddenly, "WAIT!" came a cry from an elf,
"This note just appeared on the post-sorting shelf!"

They all crowded round it, out there in the cold,
A letter so old it was starting to mould . . .

Dear Father Christmas,

I've wished for a gift on the great Northern Star
And I know my home Wonderland lies very far,
But I hope my wish finds you, out there in the snow.
You're my very last hope – please!
(My parents said no!)

Love,
The Princess of Hearts

(P.T.O for a map to Wonderland and my castle.)

"Galloping baubles!" St Nick tugged his beard.
"To be giftless at Christmas, it's worse than I feared!
To the Princess's castle we'll fly first tonight!
Set course to Wonderland, Rudolph - take flight!"

But Dancer cried out, "Oh St Nick, are you mad?
Have you not heard of Alice? The whole place is bad!"
"I agree!" chimed in Prancer, "I've heard there's a cat
That smiles at you weirdly — you KNOW I hate that!"

"We won't leave her giftless – it's Christmas! Let's go!"

So they sped through the night with a grumbly, "Ho-ho!"

They flew at full speed all that very long way,
(It's a quick trip by rabbit hole, AGES by sleigh.)

They silently crept 'cross the Princess's roof,
Then squashed down the chimney by foot and by hoof.

But no stockings were hung by the chimney with care.
No tree draped with tinsel. No treats by the stair.
"No mince pies!" Vixen frowned. "Not one candy-cane stick.
Not even a carrot! This must be a trick!"

As they stood on the hearth, St Nick scratching his head,
Somebody upstairs gently slipped from her bed . . .

"What cheek!" hissed the Queen. "Who in Wonder is that?
How dare he stand there in that red bobble hat!"
She hopped up and down, her whole face turning red,

Then she bellowed,

"OI YOU! – I say,

OFF WITH YOUR HEAD!"

Now St Nick will say fighting is never the answer,
But the same can't be said of his chief reindeer, Prancer,
Who (though on his absolute last final warning
Since biting four elves on their bottoms that morning),
CHARGED at the Queen and with all of his might . . .

Shoved her out of the window and into the night!

"Great jingle bells, Prancer!" St Nick clutched his hat
And they ran for the door but tripped over the cat!

They stumbled

and tumbled

and crashed
with a clatter . . .

Into a tea party with Hare and Mad Hatter.

"Guests!" they both cheered. "Drink a tart, eat a drink!"
"Not that one," said Mousey. "Those buns make you shrink . . ."

EAT ME

A dizzy St Nick said, "We really can't stay.
We've a gift to deliver — before Christmas Day!"

"Fried tea leaves!" gulped Hatter. "You're mad as Aunt Fred!
You can't say that word here; we'll all lose our head!"

"Our Princess of Hearts grew up angry," Hare sniffed.
"She's a Queen who HATES Christmas — she won't want a gift!"

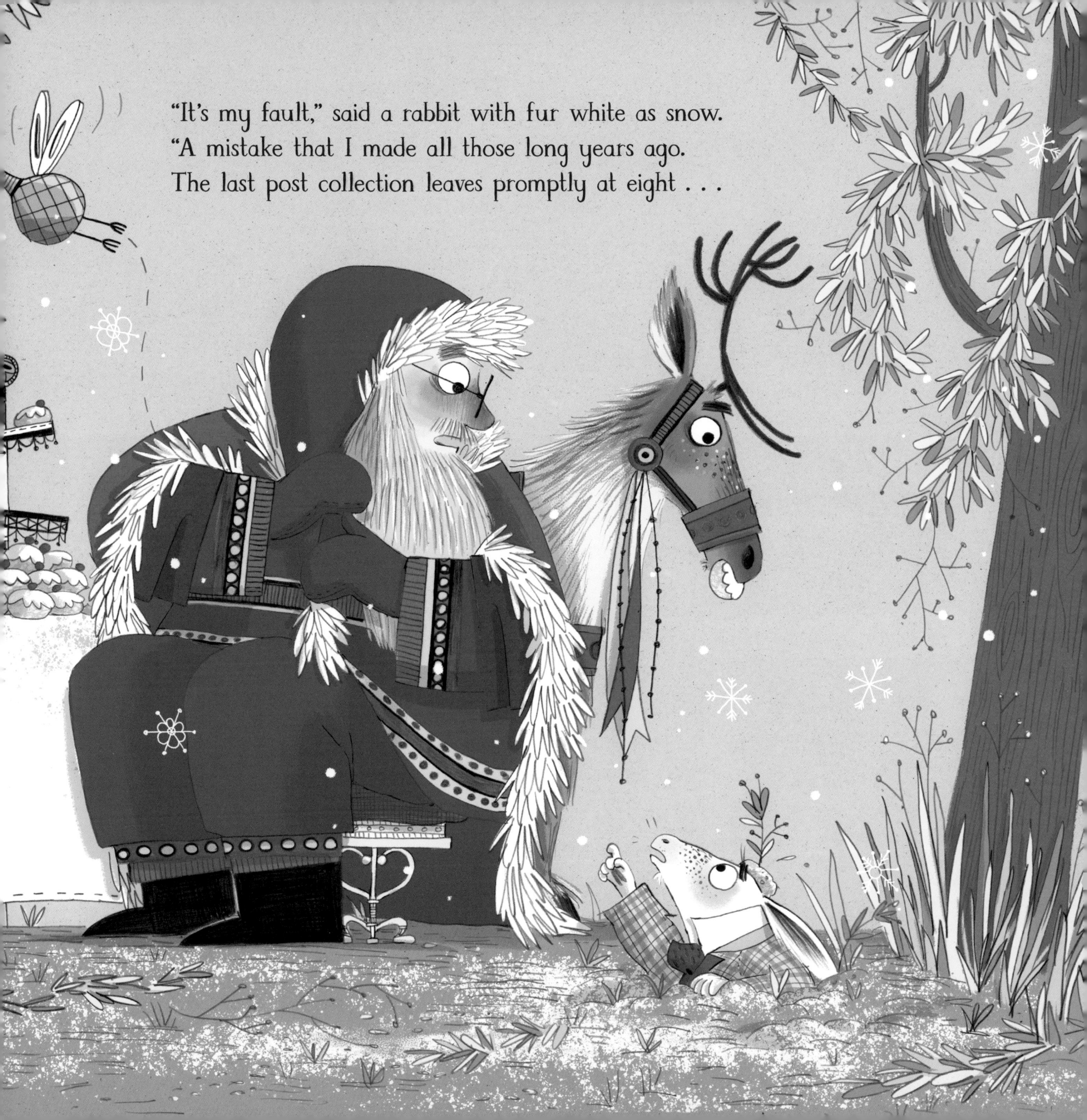

"It's my fault," said a rabbit with fur white as snow.
"A mistake that I made all those long years ago.
The last post collection leaves promptly at eight . . .

. . . And I'm sorry to say — oh dear me — I was LATE!

She was frumious! Whiffling! Then each passing year
She banned presents, then tinsel, mince pies and good cheer."

But then, "OFF WITH THEIR HEADS!" shrieked the Queen with delight.
She was back, red as jam in the brillig moonlight.

"OH-NO-HO-HO-HO!" St Nick clutched his round belly,
Which wobbled and bounced like a bowlful of jelly.
"What's that?" the Queen pointed at St Nick's red mitten,
Then slowly remembered the letter she'd written.

Her lip twitched and sorely the Queen of Hearts smiled,
For the first time since she was a very small child.

She beamed as she snatched for the red ribbon roll . . .
But it VANISHED and left a small lump of black coal.

"CHANGE IT BACK!" the Queen cried, but St Nick shook his head.
"He can't. Only you can do that," Rudolph said.

"But HOW do I do it?" the Queen of Hearts whined.
"With the first rule of Christmas," said Vixen, "Be kind."

So that night the Queen swore she'd be kind, she'd be good.
Be as nice as a Wonderland queen ever could.

She'd chop no more heads, she would share, never snatch.
And the coal changed, like magic, to a pet . . .

Bandersnatch!

Then as if by a spell, snowflakes swirled through the night
And Wonderland twinkled with warm festive light.

With Christmas restored, St Nick sprang to his sleigh,
Lots more stockings to fill before dawn Christmas Day.
He gave a warm shout as they galloped from sight . . .

"Happy Christmas to all! And to all, a goodnight!"